This sakhi book belongs to:

....

This book was devised, designed and completed by volunteers from Sikh History And Religious Education (S.H.A.R.E.)

Illustrations by Cristian Rodriguez.

SHARE

Published by Sikh History and Religious Education

Registered Charity Number: 1120428

Khalsa@sharecharityuk.com

Dedicated to those that selflessly served others with the basic human right to food, water and love.

Mata Khivi Jee was the wife of the second Guru of the Sikhs, Guru Angad Dev Jee. She was born in the village Sangar in the year 1506.

Her Mother was Karan Devi and her father was Devi Chand.

Mata Khivi Jee married Bhai Lehna Jee in 1519. Bhai Lehna Jee was a devout follower of Durga.
All the people in the village started to follow Bhai Lehna Jee and learn about Durga from Him. He was very popular.

Mata Jee had four children. Their names were Bhai Dasu, Bibi Amro, Bibi Anokhi and Bhai Datu.

After Bibi Amro had been born, Bhai Lehna Jee went for His annual religious pilgrimage.

On the way, he met Guru Nanak Dev Jee, the founder of the Sikh faith.

After many years of service at Kartarpur, Bhai Lehna Jee received Charan Amrit and Naam. He became a true Sikh and continued to serve Guru Nanak Dev Jee day and night with lots of love.

As Bhai Lehna Jee was living so far away from Mata Khivi Jee, the local people started to bully Mata Jee and said that Her husband was following the wrong path.

However, Mata Jee had a lot of faith and trust in Bhai Lehna Jee and ignore the local people.

Mata Jee learnt about Sikhi from her husband and embraced it wholeheartedly.

When Mata Jee's husband Bhai Lehna Jee became the second Guru of the Sikhs, He was renamed Guru Angad Dev Jee.

People would come to see Guru Jee day and night and Mata Jee treated everyone with love and respect.

Mata Khivi Jee was put in charge of the Guru Ka Langar.

Guru Ka Langar is free vegetarian food. It was started by Guru Nanak Dev Jee. Even today, Sikhs give free food to all.

Mata Jee only used the very best ingredients for the Guru Ka Langar. She never let anyone leave without eating from the Guru Ka Langar.

Mata Khivi Jee would ensure that everyone would recite God's name, Vaheguru, when preparing the Guru Ka Langar.
This way, Guru Ka Langar would be filled with love and positive energy.

Mata Jee moulded the Guru Ka Langar and showed us how important is it to recite naam when cooking and serving anyone.

Her daughter Bibi Amro Jee would recite the shabads of Guru Nanak Dev Jee; this led a man named Amar Das to visit her father, Guru Angad Dev Jee.

After this meeting, Amar Das did seva for Guru Angad Dev Jee for 12 years and was eventually given the Guruship at the age of 73. He became the third Guru of the Sikhs and was known as Guru Amar Das Jee.

Mata Khivi Jee continued to manage the Guru Ka Langar during the Guruship of three Guru's.

These three Guru's were called Guru Amar Das Jee, Guru Ram Das Jee and Guru Arjun Dev Jee.

Mata Khivi Jee is the only woman to be named in Sri Guru Granth Sahib Jee.

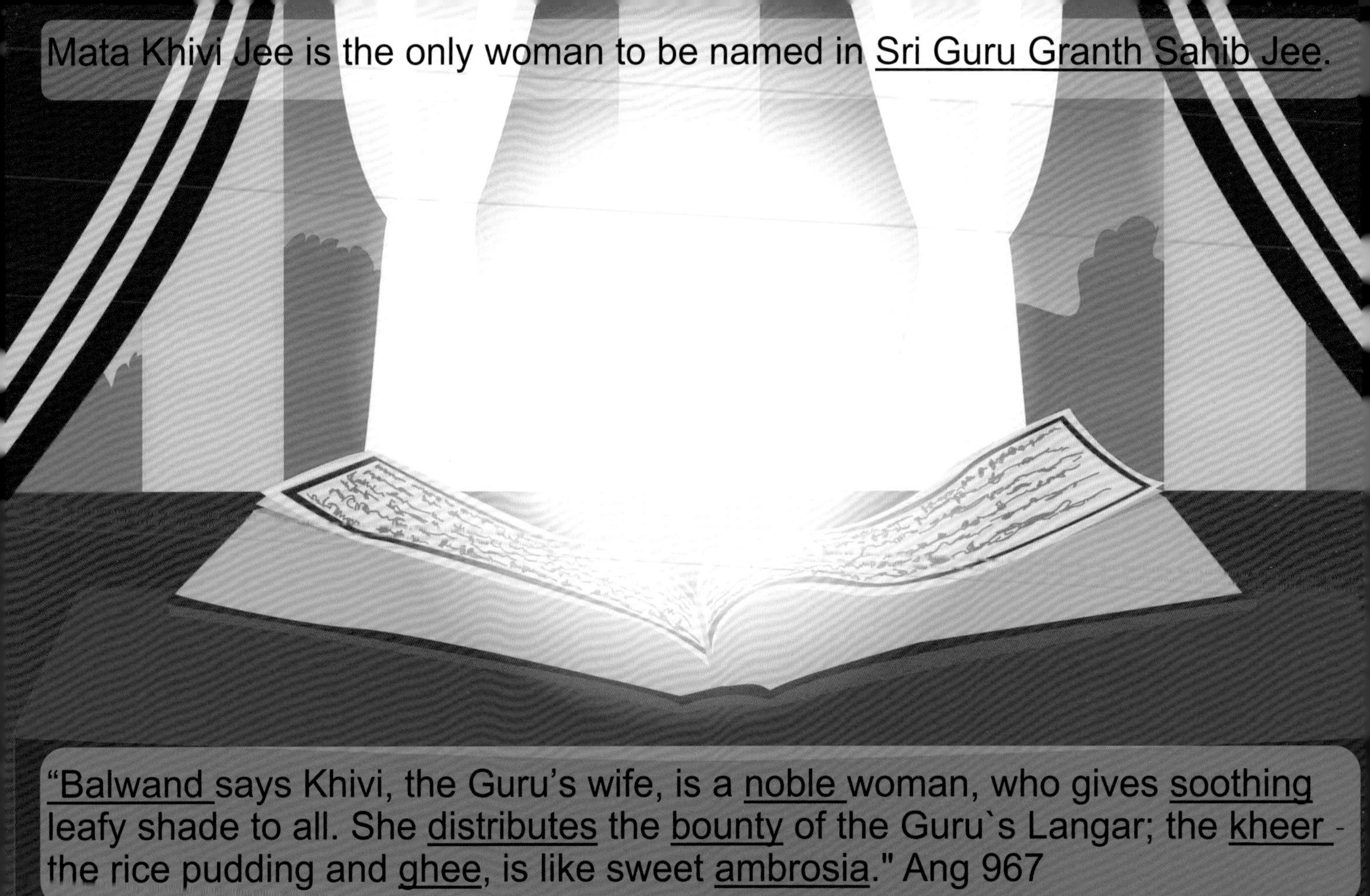

"Balwand says Khivi, the Guru's wife, is a noble woman, who gives soothing leafy shade to all. She distributes the bounty of the Guru`s Langar; the kheer - the rice pudding and ghee, is like sweet ambrosia." Ang 967

Next time you are preparing any food, try to recite God's name and imagine the positive energy flowing into the food. Look at those yummy fruit kebabs!

Mata Khivi Jee taught us to trust Guru Jee and believe in everything Guru Jee does for us.

Mata Khivi Jee taught us to love
everyone, no matter what they look
like or where they are from.

Lets See what you learnt!

1. What was the name of Mata Khivi Jee's husband before He become the Guru?

   ____

2. What was the name of Mata Jee's daughter who took Amar Das to Guru Angad Dev Jee?

   ____

3. Where did Mata Jee's husband go when He met Guru Nanak Dev Jee?

   ____

4. What was Mata Jee in charge of when her Husband become the Guru?

   ____

5. How many Gurus did Mata Jee serve?

   ____

WELL DONE!

Glossary

Amar Das: The third Guru of the Sikhs before becoming the Guru
Ambrosia: (Nectar) The drink that confers immortality (Amrit)
Annual: Occuring once a year
Balwand: Bhagat who followed Sikhi and who's shabads were added to Sri Guru Granth Sahib Jee
Bhai Lehna Jee: The second Guru of the Sikhs before becoming the Guru
Bounty: a reward, prize, bonus given
Bully: To harm or intimidate another person
Charan Amrit: Holy Amrit given from the feet of the Lord
Devout: Totally committed to a cause or belief
Distributes: To give or share
Energy: Strength required for sustained physical or mental activity. Spiritual energy is just as strong.
Faith: Complete trust or confidence in someone or something
Founder: Person who establishes an institution or settlement
Ghee: Natural Butter
Guru: Gu - Dark Ru—light (darkness into Light)
Guru Amar Das Jee: Third Guru of the Sikhs
Guru Angad Dev Jee: Second Guru of the Sikhs
Guru Arjun Dev Jee: Fifth Guru of the Sikhs
Imagine: Form a mental image or concept of

Ingredients: Foods that are combined to make a particular dish
Kartarpur: Town in (now) Pakistan where Guru Nanak Dev Jee lived
Khadur: Town in Punjab where Guru Angad Dev Jee lived before finding Sikhi
Kheer: Rice Pudding
Mata Khivi Jee: Wife of the second Guru of the Sikhs
Moulded: influence the formation or development
Naam: Gods Naam. For Sikhs its Vaheguru
Noble: Having or showing fine personal qualities or high moral principle
Paath: Prayers
Pilgrimage: Journey to a place of particular interest or significance
Positive: Happy, confident, helpful, encouraging
Recitation/recite: Repeat aloud
Religious: Relating to or believing in a religion
Sangar: Town in India, where Mata Khivi Jee was born
Sangat: Company of the holy, the body of people who meet religiously
Service: Seva—Serve or look after people/animals without reward
Sikhs: Learner, someone who follows the teachings of Sri Guru Granth Sahib
Sri Guru Granth Sahib Jee: Eternal Guru / leader of the Sikhs
Vaheguru: Wonderful God
Vegetarian: Diet that does not include animals or animal products
Wholeheartedly: completely and sincerely devoted to someone or something
Wise: showing experience, knowledge, and good judgement